Sonny's
Long Walk Home

written by
Deya Jacobs-Adams

illustrated by
Catherine Suvorova

To Calyn, Jordann, my bonus mom Janee, and in
memory of my parents Dr. Jayel and Joyce Jacobs.

All rights reserved. Published by Storybook Genius, LLC.

STORYBOOK
GENIUS PUBLISHING
sbgpublishing.com

Book
Design by
yipjar.com

It is a sunny spring afternoon as third grader Sonny Willis finishes his last assignment on the board.

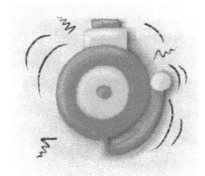

The three o'clock bell rings and it is time to go home!

"Sonny, your mom sent a note for you," Mrs. Kiser says as she hands Sonny the note.

Sonny,
I won't be able to
pick you up from
school today, so go ahead
and walk home.
Love,
MOM

It is a beautiful day so Sonny
is happy to walk home, until...

...he realizes he doesn't have his glasses.

Sonny checks his backpack
to see if his glasses are
in there. "Oh no, I must
have left them in my desk!"

Sonny begins to wonder how he will
be able to see without his glasses.

Then he remembers what his Mom and Dad always tells him when he is afraid.
"You're a big boy and more than anything you're a Willis."

"I can make it without my glasses," he says, as he
continues on his long walk home.

Things appear to be going great for
Sonny until he turns down Jacobs Street.

Standing in front of him is a huge octopus with eight legs!

Sonny's heart races, "**KUPLUMP, KUPLUMP, KUPLUMP,**" as he gets closer. "It's going to grab me!"

"WHAT AM I GOING TO DO! I have to think fast before he squirts ink on me!"
"I know, I know, I know what to do. On the count of three I'll run
in zigzags really fast past it so it won't be able to catch me!"

"One, two, three...here I go!"

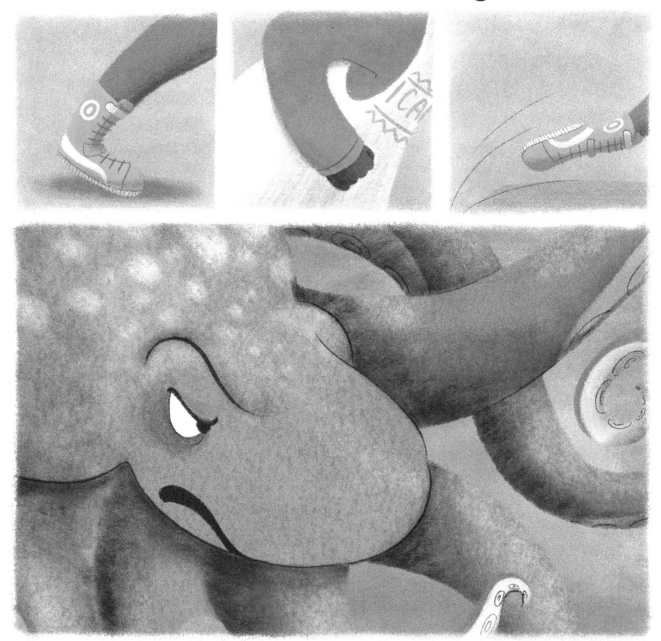

"Whew, that was close,"
Sonny says as he stops
and looks up.

"Oh, silly me! It's only a
Weeping Willow tree."
Sonny laughs and
keeps on going.

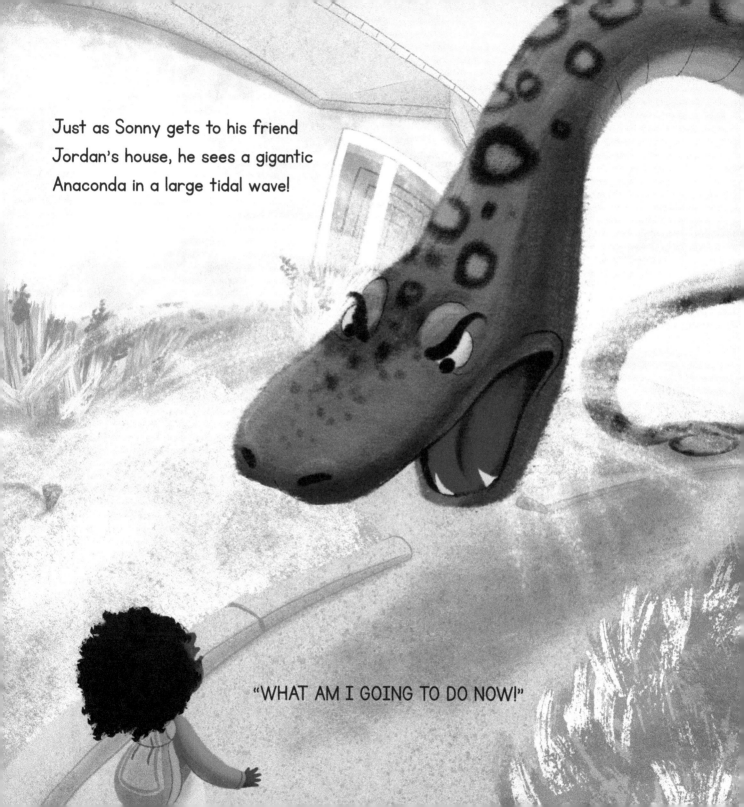

Just as Sonny gets to his friend
Jordan's house, he sees a gigantic
Anaconda in a large tidal wave!

"WHAT AM I GOING TO DO NOW!"

"I know...on the count of three I'll hold my breath and swim really fast!"

"One, two, three...here I go!"

As Sonny passes the gigantic Anaconda monster, he feels gentle drops of water.
"Oh, silly me!

It's only a hose and a water sprinkler!"

Sonny laughs and keeps on going.

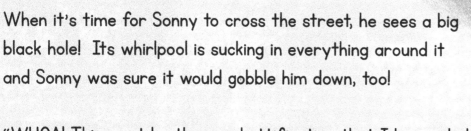

When it's time for Sonny to cross the street, he sees a big black hole! Its whirlpool is sucking in everything around it and Sonny was sure it would gobble him down, too!

"WHOA! This must be the spaghettification that I learned about in science class. I don't want to be anywhere near it!"

"OK, OK, on the count of three I'll take a great big leap over it to avoid being sucked into it!"

"One, two, three...here I go!"

As Sonny's jump puts him over the big black hole, he sees more clearly what is below his feet.

"Oh, silly me! It's only a manhole!" Sonny laughs and keeps on going.

With just a few more streets to go, Sonny decides to take a shortcut and climbs Mr. Smith's fence. To his surprise, a Siberian tiger is on the top rail taking an afternoon nap.

"OH MAN, HOW CAN THIS BE?
IF HE WAKES UP, HE WILL EAT ME!"

"I know, I'll sneak past him silently counting to three!"
Sonny counts, "One, two, three," to himself as he tiptoes past.

Sonny sneaks by the tiger and sees that
it is Mr. Smith's Bengal cat, Oscar!

"Oh boy, I never knew how much I needed my glasses!"
Sonny laughs and keeps going.

Suddenly, Sonny sees a swarm of mammoth mosquitoes coming to attack him. "What am I going to do? I don't want to be bitten and scratch all night!"

"I know. I'll close my eyes, count to three and hold so still that they won't see me! But before Sonny could count to three...

"The mammoth mosquitoes are landing on me!"

"Wait...that tickles, that is not a bite," Sonny says, as he opens his eyes to find a group of beautiful butterflies flying around him. Sonny laughs and keeps going.

During his final block home, Sonny passes his neighborhood park and he sees a flying saucer coming right for him.

"REALLY? Are you kidding me? I just can't catch a break.
I don't want the aliens to take me. I've made it this far!
I know, I'll count to three and duck down under this tree."

"One, two, three, duck!"

Sonny springs up from under the tree to clearly see his friends Ethan and Josh
throwing a Frisbee! Sonny laughs at himself, waves hello and then keeps going.

Sonny finally makes it to his front gate and is greeted by a fire-breathing dragon!

"Bring it, dragon! I've had enough and I'm not afraid! I'll take you down on the count of three!

"One, two...

...but before Sonny could count to three,
the smoke begins to clear and he sees his dad.

"Dad, I'm glad to SEE you!"

"Hey son, you're just in time to eat!
Let's go inside and get washed up!" says Dad.

"Honey, I knew you could do it," says Mom.
"Where are your glasses? Did you have any problems?"

"Nah, I'm a big boy and more than anything—I'm a Willis,"
he says as he hugs his parents tight.

CPSIA information can be obtained
at www.ICGtesting.com
Printed in the USA
LVHW011644030621
689201LV00001B/3